FOR A LOVED ONE

Heidi

Love, Mom

THE

HOLLY TREE

CHARLES DICKENS

CLARKSON POTTER/PUBLISHERS

NEW YORK

PUBLISHED BY CLARKSON N. POTTER, INC., 201 EAST 50TH STREET,
NEW YORK, NEW YORK 10022. MEMBER OF THE CROWN PUBLISHING GROUP.

RANDOM HOUSE, INC. NEW YORK, TORONTO, LONDON, SYDNEY, AUCKLAND.

CLARKSON N. POTTER, POTTER, AND COLOPHON
ARE TRADEMARKS OF CLARKSON N. POTTER, INC.

ORIGINALLY PUBLISHED IN GREAT BRITAIN BY
EBURY PRESS LIMITED IN 1994

MANUFACTURED IN HONG KONG
DESIGN BY CARROLL DEMPSEY & THIRKELL LTD
TYPESET BY SX COMPOSING LTD

ISBN 0-517-79980-4

10 9 8 7 6 5 4 3 2 1

FIRST AMERICAN EDITION

I have kept one secret in the course of my life. I am a bashful man. Nobody would suppose it, nobody ever does suppose it, nobody ever did suppose it, but I am naturally a bashful man. This is the secret which I have never breathed until now.

I might greatly move the reader by some account of the innumerable places I have not been to, the innumerable people I have not called upon or received, the innumerable social evasions I have been guilty of, solely because I am by original constitution and character a bashful man. But I will leave the reader unmoved, and proceed with the object before me.

That object is to give a plain account of my travels and discoveries in the Holly-Tree Inn; in which place of good entertainment for man and beast I was once snowed up.

It happened in the memorable year when I parted for ever from Angela Leath, whom I was shortly to have married, on making the discovery that she preferred my bosom friend. From our school-days I had freely admitted Edwin, in my own mind, to be far superior to myself; and, though I was grievously wounded at heart,

I felt the preference to be natural, and tried to forgive them both. It was under these circumstances that I resolved to go to America – on my way to the devil.

Communicating my discovery neither to Angela nor to Edwin, but resolving to write each of them an affecting letter conveying my blessing and forgiveness, which the steam-tender for shore should carry to the post when I myself should be bound for the New World, far beyond recall – I say, locking up my grief in my own breast, and consoling myself as I could with the prospect of being generous, I quietly left all I held dear, and started on the desolate journey I have mentioned.

The dead winter-time was in full dreariness when I left my chambers for ever, at five o'clock in the morning. I had shaved by candle-light, of course, and was miserably cold, and experienced that general all-pervading sensation of getting up to be hanged which I have usually found inseparable from untimely rising under such circumstances.

How well I remember the forlorn aspect of Fleet-street when I came out of the Temple! The street-lamps flickering in the gusty north-east wind, as if the very gas was contorted with cold; the white-topped houses; the bleak, star-lighted sky; the market people and other early stragglers, trotting to circulate their almost frozen blood; the hospitable light and warmth of the few coffee-shops and public-houses that were open for such customers; the hard, dry, frosty rime with which the air was charged (the wind had already beaten it into every crevice), and which lashed my face like a steel whip.

It wanted nine days to the end of the month, and end of the year. The Post-office packet for the United States was to depart from Liverpool, weather permitting, on the first of the ensuing month, and I had the intervening time on my hands. I had taken this into consideration, and had resolved to make a visit to a certain spot (which I need not name) on the farther borders of Yorkshire. It was endeared to me by my having first seen Angela at a farmhouse in that place, and my melancholy was gratified by the idea of taking a wintry leave of it before my expatriation. I ought to explain that, to avoid being sought out before my resolution should have been rendered irrevocable by being carried into full effect, I had written to Angela over night, in my usual manner, lamenting that urgent business, of which she should know all particulars by-and-by, took me unexpectedly away from her for a week or ten days.

There was no Northern Railway at that time, and in its place there were stage-coaches; which I occasionally find myself, in common with some other people, affecting to lament now, but which everybody dreaded as a very serious penance then. I had secured the box-seat on the fastest of these, and my business in Fleet-street was to get into a cab with my portmanteau, so to make the best of my way to the Peacock at Islington, where I was to join this coach. But when one of our Temple watchmen, who carried my portmanteau into Fleet-street for me, told me about the huge blocks of ice that had for some days past been floating in the river having closed up in the night and made a walk from the Temple Gardens over to the Surrey shore, I began to ask myself the question whether the box-seat would not be likely to put a sudden and frosty end to my unhappiness. I was heart-broken, it is true, and yet I was not quite so far gone as to wish to be frozen to death.

When I got up to the Peacock, – where I found everybody drinking hot purl, in self-preservation, – I asked if there were an inside seat to spare. I then discovered that, inside or out, I was the only passenger. This gave me still a livelier idea of the great inclemency of the weather, since that coach always loaded particularly well. However, I took a little purl (which I found uncommonly good), and got into the coach. When I was seated they built me up with straw to the waist, and, conscious of making a rather ridiculous appearance, I began my journey.

It was still dark when we left the Peacock. For a little while, pale, uncertain ghosts of houses and trees appeared and vanished, and then it was hard, black frozen day. People were lighting their fires; smoke was mounting straight up high into the rarefied air; and we were rattling for Highgate Archway over the hardest ground I have ever heard the ring of iron shoes on. As we got into the country everything seemed to have grown old and gray. The roads, the trees, thatched roofs of cottages and homesteads, the ricks in the farmers' yards. Outdoor work was abandoned, horse-troughs at roadside inns were frozen hard, no stragglers lounged about, doors were close shut, little turnpike houses had blazing fires inside, and children (even turnpike people have children, and seem to like them) rubbed the frost from the little panes of glass with their chubby arms, that their bright eyes might catch a glimpse of the solitary coach going by. I don't know when the snow began to set in; but I know that we were changing horses somewhere when I heard the guard remark 'that the old lady up in the sky was picking her geese pretty hard to-day.' Then, indeed, I found the white down falling fast and thick.

I forget now where we were at noon on the second day, and where we ought to have been; but I know that we were scores of miles behind-hand, and that our case was growing worse every hour. The drift was becoming prodigiously deep; land-marks were getting snowed out; the road and the fields were all one; instead of having fences and hedgerows to guide us, we went crunching on over an unbroken surface of ghastly white that might sink beneath us at any moment and drop us down a whole hillside.

When we came in sight of a town, it looked, to my fancy, like a large drawing on a slate, with abundance of slate-pencil expended on the churches and houses where the snow lay thickest. When we came within a town, and found the church clocks all stopped, the dial-faces choked with snow, and the inn-signs blotted out, it seemed as if the whole place was overgrown with white moss. As to the coach, it was a mere snowball; similarly, the men and boys who ran along beside us to the town's end, turning our clogged wheels and encouraging our horses, were men and boys of snow; and the bleak, wild solitude to which they at last dismissed us was a snowy Sahara. One would have thought this enough: notwithstanding which, I pledge my word that it snowed and snowed, and still it snowed, and never left off snowing.

We performed Auld Lang Syne the whole day; seeing nothing, out of towns and villages, but the track of stoats, hares, and foxes, and sometimes of birds. At nine o'clock at night, on a Yorkshire moor, a cheerful burst from our horn, and a welcome sound of talking, with a glimmering and moving about of lanterns, roused me from my drowsy state. I found that we were going to change.

They helped me out, and I said to a waiter, whose bare head became as white as King Lear's in a single minute, 'What inn is this?'

'The Holly-Tree, Sir,' said he.

'Upon my word, I believe,' said I, apologetically to the guard and coachman, 'that I must stop here.'

Now, the landlord and the landlady, and the ostler,

and the postboy, and all the stable authorities, had already asked the coachman, to the wide-eyed interest of all the rest of the establishment, if he meant to go on. The coachman had already replied, 'Yes, he'd take her through it,' – meaning by her the coach – 'if so be as George would stand by him.' George was the guard, and he had already sworn that he *would* stand by him. So the helpers were already getting the horses out.

My declaring myself beaten, after this parley, was not an announcement without preparation. Indeed, but for the way to the announcement being smoothed by the parley, I more than doubt whether, as an innately bashful man, I should have had the confidence to make it. As it was, it received the approval even of the guard and coachman. Therefore, with many confirmations of my inclining, and many remarks from one bystander to another, that the gentleman could go for'ard by the mail to-morrow, whereas to-night he would only be froze, and where was the good of a gentleman being froze, – ah, let alone buried alive (which latter clause was added by a humorous helper as a joke at my expense, and was extremely well received), I saw my portmanteau got out stiff like a frozen body; did the handsome thing by the guard and coachman; wished them good-night and a prosperous journey; and, a little ashamed of myself, after all, for leaving them to fight it out alone, followed the landlord, landlady, and waiter of the Holly-Tree upstairs.

I thought I had never seen such a large room as that into which they showed me. It had five windows, with dark red curtains, that would have absorbed the light of a general illumination; and there were complications of drapery at the top of the curtains, that went wandering about the wall in a most extraordinary manner. I asked for a smaller room, and they told me there was no smaller room. They could screen me in, however, the landlord said. They brought a great old japanned screen, with natives (Japanese, I suppose) engaged in a variety of idiotic pursuits all over it; and left me roasting whole before an immense fire.

My bedroom was some quarter of a mile off, up a great staircase at the end of a long gallery; and nobody knows what a misery this is to a bashful man who would rather not meet people on the stairs. It was the grimmest room I have ever had the nightmare in; and all the furniture, from the four posts of the bed to the two old silver candlesticks, was tall, high-shouldered, and spindle-waisted. Below, in my sitting-room, if I looked round my screen, the wind rushed at me like a mad bull; if I stuck to my armchair, the fire scorched me to the colour of a new brick. The chimneypiece was very high and there was a bad glass – what I may call a wavy glass – above it, which, when I stood up, just showed me my anterior phrenological developments – and these never look well, in any subject cut short off at the eyebrows. If I stood with my back to the fire, a gloomy vault of darkness above and beyond the screen insisted on being looked at; and, in its dim remoteness, the drapery of the ten curtains of the five windows went twisting and creeping about, like a nest of gigantic worms.

I suppose that what I observe in myself must be observed by some other men of similar character in *themselves*; therefore I am emboldened to mention that, when I travel, I never arrive at a place but I immediately want to go away from it. Before I had finished my supper of broiled fowl and mulled port, I had impressed upon the waiter in detail my arrangements for departure in the morning. Breakfast and bill at eight. Fly at nine. Two horses, or, if needful, even four.

Tired though I was, the night appeared about a week long. In oases of nightmare, I thought of Angela, and felt more depressed than ever by the reflection that I was on the shortest road to Gretna Green. What had I to do with Gretna Green? I was not going that way to the devil, but by the American route, I remarked in my bitterness.

In the morning I found that it was snowing still, that it had snowed all night, and that I was snowed up. Nothing could get out of that spot on the moor, or could come in, until the road had been cut out by labourers from the market-town. When they might cut their way to the Holly-Tree nobody could tell me.

It was now Christmas-eve. I should have had a dismal Christmas time of it anywhere, and consequently that did not so much matter; still, being snowed up was like dying of frost, a thing I had not bargained for. I felt very lonely. Yet I could no more have proposed to the landlord and landlady to admit me to their society (though I should have liked it very much) than I could have asked them to present me with a piece of plate. Here my great secret, the real bashfulness of my character, is to be observed. Like most bashful men, I judge of other people as if they were bashful too. Besides being far too shamefaced to make the proposal myself, I really had a delicate misgiving that it would be in the last degree disconcerting to them.

Trying to settle down, therefore, in my solitude, I first of all asked what books there were in the house. The waiter brought me a *Book of Roads*, two or three old Newspapers, a little Song-Book, terminating in a collection of Toasts and Sentiments, a little Jest-Book, an odd volume of *Peregrine Pickle* and the *Sentimental Journey*. I knew every word of the two last already, but I read them through again, then tried to hum all the songs (Auld Lang Syne was among them); went entirely through the jokes – in which I found a fund of melancholy adapted to my state of mind; proposed all the toasts, enunciated all the sentiments, and mastered the papers. The latter had nothing in them but a stock of advertisements, a meeting about a country rate, and a highway robbery. As I am a greedy reader, I could not make this supply hold out until night; it was exhausted by teatime. Being then entirely cast upon my own resources, I got through an hour in considering what to do next. . .

A desperate idea came into my head. Under any other circumstance I should have rejected it; but, in the strait at which I was, I held it fast. Could I so far over-come the inherent bashfulness which withheld me from the landlord's table and the company I might find there, as to call up the Boots, and ask him to take a chair, – and something in a liquid form, – and talk to me? I could. I would. I did.

SECOND BRANCH. THE BOOTS

Where had he been in his time? he repeated, when I asked him the question. Lord, he had been everywhere! And what had he been? Bless you, he had been every-thing you could mention a'most!

Seen a good deal? Why, of course, he had. I should say so, he could assure me, if I only knew about the twentieth part of what had come in *his* way. Why, it would be easier for him, he expected, to tell what he hadn't seen than what he had. Ah! A deal, it would.

What was the curiousest thing he had seen? Well! He didn't know. He couldn't momently name what was the curiousest thing he had seen, – unless it was a Unicorn, – and he see *him* once at a Fair. But supposing a young gentleman not eight year old was to run away with a fine young woman of seven, might I think *that* a queer start? Certainly. Then that was a start as he himself had had his blessed eyes on, and he had cleaned the shoes they run away in – and they was so little that he couldn't get his hand into 'em.

Master Harry Walmers' father, you see, he lived at the Elmses, down away by Shooter's Hill there, six or seven miles from Lunnon. He was a gentleman of spirit, and good-looking, and held his head up when he walked, and had what you may call Fire about him. He wrote poetry, and he rode, and he ran, and he cricketed, and he danced, and he acted, and he done it all equally beautiful. He was uncommon proud of Master Harry as was his only child; but he didn't spoil him neither. He was a gentleman that had a will of his own and a eye of his own, and that would be minded. Consequently, though he had made quite a companion of the fine bright boy, and was delighted to see him so fond of reading his fairy books, and was never tired of hearing him say my name is Norval, or hearing him sing his songs about Young May Moons is beaming love, and When he as adores thee has left but the name, and that; still he kept the command over the child, and the child *was* a child, and it's to be wished more of 'em was!

How did Boots happen to know all this? Why, through being under-gardener. Of course he couldn't be under-gardener, and be always about, in the summer-time, near the windows on the lawn, a-mowing, and sweeping, and weeding, and pruning and this and that, without getting acquainted with the ways of the family. Even supposing Master Harry hadn't come to him one morning early, and said, 'Cobbs, how should you spell Norah, if you was asked?' and then began cutting it in print all over the fence.

He couldn't say he had taken particular notice of children before that; but really it was pretty to see them two mites a-going about the place together, deep in love. And the courage of the boy! Bless your soul, he'd have throwed off his little hat, and tucked up his little sleeves, and gone in at a Lion, he would, if they happened to meet one, and she had been frightened of him. One day he stops, along with her, where Boots was hoeing weeds in the gravel, and says, speaking up, 'Cobbs,' he says, 'I like *you*.' 'Do you, Sir? I'm proud to hear it.' 'Yes, I do, Cobbs. Why do I like you, do you think, Cobbs?' 'Don't know, Master Harry, I am sure.' 'Because Norah likes you, Cobbs.' 'Indeed, Sir? That's very gratifying.' 'Gratifying, Cobbs? It's better than millions of the brightest diamonds to be liked by Norah.' 'Certainly, Sir,' 'You're going away, ain't you, Cobbs?' 'Yes, Sir,' 'Would you like another situation, Cobbs?' 'Well, Sir, I shouldn't object, if it was a good 'un.' 'Then, Cobbs,' says he, 'you shall be our Head Gardener when we are married.' And he tucks her, in her little sky-blue mantle, under his arm, and walks away.

Boots could assure me that it was better than a picter, and equal to a play, to see them babies, with their long, bright, curling hair, their sparkling eyes, and their beautiful light tread, a-rambling about the garden, deep in love. Boots was of opinion that the birds believed they was birds, and kept up with 'em, singing to please 'em. Sometimes they would creep under the Tulip-tree, and would sit there with their arms round one another's necks, and their soft cheeks touching, a-reading about the Prince and the Dragon, and the good and bad enchanters, and the king's fair daughter. Sometimes he would hear them planning about having a house in a forest, keeping bees and a cow, and living entirely on milk and honey. Once he came upon them by the pond, and heard Master Harry say, 'Adorable Norah, kiss me, and say you love me to distraction, or I'll jump in head foremost.' And Boots made no question he would have done it if she hadn't complied. On the whole, Boots said it had a tendency to make him feel as if he was in love himself – only he didn't exactly know who with.

'Cobbs,' said Master Harry, one evening, when Cobbs was watering the flowers, 'I am going on a visit, this present Midsummer, to my grandmamma's at York.'

'Are you indeed, Sir? I hope you'll have a pleasant time. I am going into Yorkshire, myself, when I leave here.'

'Are you going to your grandmamma's, Cobbs?'

'No, Sir. I haven't got such a thing.'

'Not as a grandmamma, Cobbs?'

'No, Sir.'

The boy looked on at the watering of the flowers for a little while, and then said, 'I shall be very glad indeed to go, Cobbs, - Norah's going.'

'You'll be all right then, Sir,' says Cobbs, 'with your beautiful sweetheart by your side.'

'Cobbs,' returned the boy, flushing, 'I never let anybody joke about it, when I can prevent them.'

'It wasn't a joke, Sir,' says Cobbs, with humility, – 'wasn't so meant.'

'I am glad of that, Cobbs, because I like you, you know, and you're going to live with us, – Cobbs!'

'Sir.'

'What do you think my grandmamma gives me when I go down there?'

'I couldn't so much as make a guess, Sir.'

'A Bank of England five-pound note, Cobbs.'

'Whew!' says Cobbs, 'that's a spanking sum of money, Master Harry.'

'A person could do a good deal with such a sum of money as that, – couldn't a person, Cobbs?'

'I believe you, Sir!'

'Cobbs,' said the boy, 'I'll tell you a secret. At Norah's house, they have been joking her about me, and pretending to laugh at our being engaged, –

pretending to make game of it, Cobbs!'

'Such, Sir,' says Cobbs, 'is the depravity of human natur.'

The boy looking exactly like his father, stood for a few minutes with his glowing face towards the sunset, and then departed with, 'Good-night, Cobbs. I'm going in.'

If I was to ask Boots how it happened that he was a-going to leave that place just at that present time, well, he couldn't rightly answer me. He did suppose he might have stayed there till now if he had been anyways inclined. But, you see, he was younger then, and he wanted change. That's what he wanted, – change. Mr. Walmers, he said to him when he gave him notice of his intentions to leave, 'Cobbs,' he says, 'have you anythink to complain of? I make the inquiry because if I find that any of my people really has anythink to complain of, I wish to make it right if I can.' 'No, Sir,' says Cobbs; 'thanking you, Sir, I find myself as well sitiwated here as I could hope to be anywheres. The truth is, Sir, that I'm a-going to seek my fortun'.' 'O, indeed Cobbs!' he says; 'I hope you may find it.' And Boots could assure me – which he did, touching his hair with his bootjack, as a salute in the way of his present calling – that he hadn't found it yet.

Well, Sir! Boots left the Elmses when his time was up, and Master Harry, he went down to the old lady's at York, which old lady would have given that child the teeth out of her head (if she had had any), she was so wrapped up in him. What does that Infant do, – for Infant you may call him and be within the mark, – but cut away from that old lady's with his Norah, on a expedition to go to Gretna Green and be married!

Sir, Boots was at this identical Holly-Tree Inn (having left it several times since to better himself, but always come back through one thing or another), when, one summer afternoon, the coach drives up, and out of the coach gets them two children. The Guard says to our Governor, 'I don't quite make out these little passengers, but the young gentleman's words was, that they was to be brought here.' The young gentleman gets out; hands his lady out; gives the Guard something for himself; says to our Governor, 'We're to stop here to-night, please. Sitting-room and two bedrooms will be required. Chops and cherry-pudding for two!' and tucks her, in her little sky-blue mantle, under his arm, and walks into the house much bolder than Brass.

Boots leaves me to judge what the amazement of that establishment was, when these two tiny creatures all alone by themselves was marched into the Angel, – much more so, when he, who had seen them without their seeing him, give the Governor his views of the expedition they was upon. 'Cobbs,' says the Governor, 'if this is so, I must set off myself to York, and quiet their friends' minds. In which case you must keep your eye upon 'em, and humour 'em, till I come back. But before I take these measures, Cobbs, I should wish you to find from themselves whether your opinion is correct.' 'Sir, to you,' says Cobbs, 'that shall be done directly.'

So Boots goes upstairs to the Angel, and there he finds Master Harry on a e-normous sofa, – immense at any time, but looking like the Great Bed of Ware, compared with him, – a-drying the eyes of Miss Norah with his pocket-hankecher. Their little legs was entirely off the ground, of course, and it really is not possible for Boots to express to me how small them children looked.

'It's Cobbs! It's Cobbs!' cried Master Harry, and comes running to him, and catching hold of his hand. Miss Norah comes running to him on t'other side and catching hold of his t'other hand, and they both jump for joy.

'I see you a-getting out, Sir,' says Cobbs. 'I thought it was you. I thought I couldn't be mistaken in your height and figure. What's the object of your journey, Sir? – Matrimonial?'

'We are going to be married, Cobbs, at Gretna Green,' returned the boy. 'We have run away on purpose. Norah has been in rather low spirits, Cobbs; but she'll be happy now we have found you to be our friend.'

'Thank you, Sir, and thank *you*, Miss,' says Cobbs, 'for your good opinion. *Did* you bring any luggage with you, Sir?'

If I will believe Boots when he gives me his word and honour upon it, the lady had got a parasol, a smelling-bottle, a round and a half of cold buttered toast, eight peppermint drops, and a hairbrush, - seemingly a doll's. The gentleman had got about half-a-dozen yards of string, a knife, three or four sheets of writing-paper folded up surprisingly small, a orange, and a Chaney mug with his name upon it.

'What may be the exact nature of your plans, Sir?' says Cobbs.

'To go on,' replied the boy, – which the courage of that boy was something wonderful! 'in the morning, and be married to-morrow.'

'Just so, Sir,' says Cobbs. 'Would it meet your views, Sir, if I was to accompany you?'

When Cobbs said this, they both jumped for joy again, and cried out, 'Oh yes, yes, Cobbs! Yes!'

'Well, Sir,' says Cobbs. 'If you will excuse my having the freedom to give an opinion, what I should recommend would be this. I'm acquainted with a pony, Sir, which, put in a pheayton that I could borrow, would take you and Mrs. Harry Walmers, Junior, (myself driving, if you approved), to the end of your journey in a very short space of time. I am not altogether sure, Sir, that this pony will be at liberty to-morrow, but even if you had to wait over to-morrow for him, it might be worth your while. As to the small account here, Sir, in case you was to find yourself running at all short, that don't signify; because I'm a part proprietor of this inn, and it could stand over.'

Boots assures me that when they clapped their hands, and jumped for joy again, and called him, 'Good Cobbs!' and, 'Dear Cobbs!' and bent across him to kiss one another in the delight of their confiding hearts, he felt himself the meanest rascal for deceiving 'em that ever was born.

'Is there anything you want just at present, Sir?' says Cobbs, mortally ashamed of himself.

'We should like some cakes after dinner,' answered Master Harry, folding his arms, putting out one leg, and looking straight at him, 'and two apples – and jam. With dinner we should like to have toast-and-water. But Norah has always been accustomed to half a glass of currant wine at dessert. And so have I.'

'It shall be ordered at the bar, Sir,' says Cobbs; and away he went.

Boots has the feeling as fresh upon him at this minute of speaking as he had then, that he would far rather have had it out in half-a-dozen rounds with the Governor than have combined with him; and that he wished with all his heart there was any impossible place where those two babies could make an impossible marriage, and live impossibly happy ever afterwards. However, as it couldn't be, he went into the Governor's plans, and the Governor set off for York in half an hour.

The way in which the women of that house – without exception – every one of 'em – married *and* single – took to that boy when they heard the story, Boots considers surprising. It was as much as he could do to keep 'em from dashing into the room and kissing him. They climbed up all sorts of places, at the risk of their lives, to look at him through a pane of glass. They was seven deep at the keyhole. They was out of their minds about him and his bold spirit.

In the evening, Boots went into the room to see how the runaway couple was getting on. The gentleman was on the window-seat, supporting the lady in his arms. She had tears upon her face, and was lying, very tired and half asleep, with her head upon his shoulder.

'Mrs. Harry Walmers, Junior, fatigued, Sir?' says Cobbs.

'Yes, she is tired, Cobbs; but she is not used to be away from home, and she has been in low spirits again. Cobbs, do you think you could bring a biffin, please?'

'I ask your pardon, Sir,' says Cobbs. 'What was it you – ?'

'I think a Norfolk biffin would rouse her, Cobbs. She is very fond of them.'

Boots withdrew in search of the required restorative, and, when he brought it in, the gentleman handed it to the lady, and fed her with a spoon, and took a little himself; the lady being heavy with sleep, and rather cross. 'What should you think, Sir,' says Cobbs, 'of a chamber candlestick?' The gentleman approved; the chambermaid went first, up the great staircase; the lady, in her sky-blue mantle followed, gallantly escorted by the gentleman; the gentleman embraced her at her door, and retired to his own apartment, where Boots softly locked him up.

Boots couldn't but feel with increased acuteness what a base deceiver he was, when they consulted him at breakfast (they had ordered sweet milk-and-water, and toast and currant jelly, overnight) about the pony. It really was as much as he could do, he don't mind confessing to me, to look them two young things in the face, and think what a wicked old father of lies he had grown up to be. Howsomever, he went on a-lying like a Trojan about the pony. He told 'em that it did so unfort'nately happen that the pony was half clipped, you see, and that he couldn't be taken out in that state, for fear it should strike to his inside. But that he'd be finished clipping in the course of the day, and that to-morrow morning at eight o'clock the pheayton would be ready. Boots's view of the whole case, looking back on it in my room, is, that Mrs. Harry Walmers, Junior, was beginning to give in. She hadn't had her hair curled when she went to bed, and she didn't seem quite up to brushing it herself, and its getting in her eyes put her out. But nothing put out Master Harry. He sat behind his breakfast-cup, a-tearing away at the jelly, as if he had been his own father.

After breakfast, Boots is inclined to consider that

they drawed soldiers – at least, he knows that many
such was found in the fireplace, all on horseback. In the
course of the morning, Master Harry rang the bell – it
was surprising how that there boy did carry on – and
said, in a sprightly way, 'Cobbs, is there any good walks
in this neighbourhood?'

'Yes, Sir,' says Cobbs. 'There's Love-lane.'

'Get out with you, Cobbs!' – that was that there
boy's expression – 'you're joking.'

'Begging your pardon, Sir,' says Cobbs, 'there really
is Love-lane. And a pleasant walk it is, and proud shall
I be to show it to yourself and Mrs. Harry Walmers,
Junior.'

'Norah, dear,' said Master Harry, 'this is curious. We
really ought to see Love-lane. Put on your bonnet, my
sweetest darling, and we will go there with Cobbs.'

Boots leaves me to judge what a beast he felt himself
to be, when the young pair told him, as they all three
jogged along together, that they had made up their
minds to give him two thousand guineas a year as head-
gardener, on accounts of his being so true a friend to
'em. Boots could have wished at the moment that the
earth would have opened and swallowed him up, he felt
so mean, with their beaming eyes a-looking at him, and
believing him. Well, Sir, he turned the conversation as
well as he could, and he took 'em down Love-lane to
the water-meadows, and there Master Harry would
have drowned himself in half a moment more, a–getting

out a water-lily for her – but nothing daunted that boy. Well, Sir, they was tired out. All being so new and strange to 'em, they was tired as tired could be. And they laid down on a bank of daisies, like the children in the wood, leastways meadows, and fell asleep.

Boots don't know – perhaps I do – but never mind, it don't signify either way – why it made a man fit to make a fool of himself to see them two pretty babies a-lying there in the clear, still, sunny day, not dreaming half so hard when they was asleep as they done when they was awake. But, Lord! when you come to think of yourself, you know, and what a game you have been up to ever since you was in your own cradle, and what a poor sort of chap you are, and how it's always either Yesterday with you, or else To-morrow, and never To-day, that's where it is.

Well, Sir, they woke up at last, and then one thing was getting pretty clear to Boots, namely, that Mrs. Harry Walmerses, Junior's, temper was on the move. When Master Harry took her round the waist, she said he 'teased her so'; and when he says, 'Norah, my young May Moon, your Harry tease you?' she tells him, 'Yes; and I want to go home!'

A biled fowl, and baked bread-and-butter pudding, brought Mrs. Walmers up a little; but Boots could have wished, he must privately own to me, to have seen her more sensible of the woice of love, and less abandoning of herself to currants. However, Master Harry, he kept up, and his noble heart was as fond as ever. Mrs. Walmers turned very sleepy about dusk and began to cry. Therefore, Mrs. Walmers went off to bed as per yesterday; and Master Harry ditto repeated.

About eleven or twelve at night comes back the Governor in a chaise, along with Mr. Walmers and a elderly lady. Mr. Walmers looks amused and very serious, both at once, and says to our missis, 'We are much indebted to you, ma'am, for your kind care of our little children, which we can never sufficiently acknowledge. Pray, ma'am, where is my boy?' Our missis says, 'Cobbs has the dear child in charge, Sir. Cobbs, show Forty!' Then he says to Cobbs, 'Ah, Cobbs, I am glad to see *you*! I understood you was here!' And Cobbs says, 'Yes, Sir. Your most obedient, Sir.'

I may be surprised to hear Boots say it, perhaps; but Boots assures me that his heart beat like a hammer, going upstairs. 'I beg your pardon, Sir,' says he, while unlocking the door; 'I hope you are not angry with Master Harry. For Master Harry is a fine boy, Sir, and will do you credit and honour.' And Boots signifies to me, that, if the fine boy's father had contradicted him in the daring state of mind in which he then was, he thinks he should have 'fetched him a crack,' and taken the consequences.

But Mr. Walmers only says, 'No, Cobbs. No, my good fellow. Thank you!' And, the door being opened, goes in.

Boots goes in too, holding the light, and he sees Mr. Walmers go up to the bedside, bend gently down, and kiss the little sleeping face. Then he stands looking at it for a minute, looking wonderfully like it (they do say he ran away with Mrs. Walmers); and then he gently shakes the little shoulder.

'Harry, my dear boy! Harry!'

Master Harry starts up and looks at him. Looks at Cobbs too. Such is the honour of that mite, that he looks at Cobbs, to see whether he has brought him into trouble.

'I am not angry, my child. I only want you to dress yourself and come home.'

'Yes, pa.'

Master Harry dresses himself quickly. His breast begins to swell when he has nearly finished, and it swells more and more as he stands, at last, a-looking at his father; his father standing a-looking at him, the quiet image of him.

'Please may I' – the spirit of that little creature, and the way he kept his rising tears down! – 'please, dear pa – may I – kiss Norah before I go?'

'You may, my child.'

So he takes Master Harry in his hand, and Boots leads the way with the candle, and they come to that other bedroom, where the elderly lady is seated by the bed, and poor little Mrs. Harry Walmers, Junior, is fast asleep. There the father lifts the child up to the pillow, and he lays his little face down for an instant by the little warm face of poor unconscious little Mrs. Harry Walmers, Junior, and gently draws it to him – a sight so touching to the chambermaids who are peeping through the door, that one of them calls out, 'It's a shame to part 'em!' But this chambermaid was always, as Boots informs me, a soft-hearted one. Not that there was any harm in that girl. Far from it.

Finally, Boots says, that's all about it. Mr. Walmers drove away in the chaise, having hold of Master Harry's hand. The elderly lady and Mrs. Harry Walmers, Junior, that was never to be (she married a Captain long afterwards, and died in India), went off next day. In conclusion, Boots put it to me whether I hold with him in two opinions: firstly, that there are not many couples on their way to be married who are half as innocent of guile as those two children; secondly, that it would be a jolly good thing for a great many couples on their way to be married, if they could only be stopped in time, and brought back separately.

THIRD BRANCH. THE BILL

I had been snowed up a whole week. The time had hung so lightly on my hands, that I should have been in great doubt of the fact but for a piece of documentary evidence that lay upon my table.

The road had been dug out of the snow on the

previous day, and the document in question was my bill. It testified emphatically to my having eaten and drunk, and warmed myself, and slept among the sheltering branches of the Holly-Tree, seven days and nights.

I had yesterday allowed the road twenty-four hours to improve itself, finding that I required that additional margin of time for the completion of my task. I had ordered my bill to be upon the table, and a chaise to be at the door, 'at eight o'clock to-morrow evening.' It was eight o'clock to-morrow evening when I buckled up my travelling writing-desk in its leather case, paid my bill, and got on my warm coats and wrappers. Of course, no time now remained for my travelling on to add a frozen tear to the icicles which were doubtless hanging plentifully about the farmhouse where I had first seen Angela. What I had to do was to get across to Liverpool by the shortest open road, there to meet my heavy baggage and embark. It was quite enough to do, and I had not an hour too much time to do it in.

I had taken leave of all my Holly-Tree friends – almost, for the time being, of my bashfulness too – and was standing for half a minute at the Inn door watching the ostler as he took another turn at the cord which tied my portmanteau on the chaise, when I saw lamps coming down towards the Holly-Tree. The road was so padded with snow that no wheels were audible; but all of us who were standing at the Inn door saw lamps coming on, and at a lively rate too, between the walls of snow that had been heaped up on either side of the track. The chambermaid instantly divined how the case stood and called to the ostler, 'Tom, this is a Gretna job!' The ostler, knowing that her sex instinctively scented a marriage, or anything in that direction, rushed up the yard bawling, 'Next four out!' and in a moment the whole establishment was thrown into commotion.

I had a melancholy interest in seeing the happy man who loved and was beloved; and therefore, instead of driving off at once, I remained at the Inn door when the fugitives drove up. A bright-eyed fellow, muffled in a mantle, jumped out so briskly that he almost over-threw me. He turned to apologise, and, by Heaven, it was Edwin!

'Charley!' said he, recoiling. 'Gracious powers, what do you do here?'

'Edwin,' said I, recoiling, 'gracious powers, what do *you* do here?' I struck my forehead as I said it, and an insupportable blaze of light seemed to shoot before my eyes.

He hurried me into the little parlour (always kept with a low fire in it and no poker), where posting company waited while their horses were putting to, and, shutting the door, said:

'Charley, forgive me!'

'Edwin!' I returned. 'Was this well? When I loved her so dearly! When I had garnered up my heart so long!' I could say no more.

He was shocked when he saw how moved I was, and made the cruel observation that he had not thought I should have taken it so much to heart.

I looked at him. I reproached him no more. But I looked at him.

'My dear, dear Charley,' said he, 'don't think ill of me, I beseech you! I know you have a right to my utmost confidence, and, believe me, you have ever had it until now. I abhor secrecy. Its meanness is intolerable to me. But I and my dear girl have observed it for your sake.'

He and his dear girl! It steeled me.

'You have observed it for my sake, Sir?' said I, wondering how his frank face could face it out so.

'Yes! – and Angela's,' said he.

I found the room reeling round in an uncertain way, like a labouring humming-top. 'Explain yourself,' said I, holding on by one hand to an armchair.

'Dear old darling Charley!' returned Edwin, in his cordial manner, 'consider! When you were going on so happily with Angela, why should I compromise you with the old gentleman by making you a party to our engagement, and (after he had declined my proposals) to our secret intention? Surely it was better that you should be able honourably to say, "He never took counsel with me, never told me, never breathed a word of it." If Angela suspected it, and showed me all the favour and support she could – God bless her for a precious creature and a priceless wife! – I couldn't help that. Neither I nor Emmeline ever told her, any more than we told you. And for the same good reason, Charley; trust me, for the same good reason, and no other upon earth!'

Emmeline was Angela's cousin. Lived with her. Had been brought up with her. Was her father's ward. Had property.

'Emmeline is in the chaise, my dear Edwin!' said I, embracing him with the greatest affection.

'My good fellow!' said he, 'do you suppose I should be going to Gretna Green without her?'

I ran out with Edwin, I opened the chaise door, I took Emmeline in my arms, I folded her to my heart. She was wrapped in soft white fur, like the snowy landscape: but was warm, and young, and lovely. I put their leaders to with my own hands, I gave the boys a five-pound note apiece, I cheered them as they drove away, I drove the other way myself as hard as I could pelt.

I never went to Liverpool, I never went to America, I went straight back to London, and I married Angela. I have never until this time, even to her, disclosed the secret of my character, and the mistrust and the mistaken journey into which it led me. When she, and they, and our eight children and their seven – I mean Edwin's and Emmeline's, whose eldest girl is old enough now to wear white for herself, and to look very like her mother in it – come to read these pages, as of course they will,

I shall hardly fail to be found out at last. Never mind! I can bear it. I began at the Holly-Tree, by idle accident, to associate the Christmas-time of the year with human interest, and with some inquiry into, and some care for, the lives of those by whom I find myself surrounded. I hope that I am none the worse for it, and that no one near me or afar off is the worse for it. And I say, may the green Holly-Tree flourish, striking its roots deep into our English ground, and having its germinating qualities carried by the birds of Heaven all over the world!